Backyard SP⚫RTS™

Inside Edge

By Michael Teitelbaum

Illustrated by Ron Zalme

Grosset & Dunlap • A Stonesong Press Book

This one's for Steven.—M.T.

A Stonesong Press Book

GROSSET & DUNLAP
Published by the Penguin Group
Penguin Group (USA) Inc., 375 Hudson Street, New York, New York 10014, USA
Penguin Group (Canada), 90 Eglinton Avenue East, Suite 700,
Toronto, Ontario M4P 2Y3, Canada
(a division of Pearson Penguin Canada Inc.)
Penguin Books Ltd., 80 Strand, London WC2R 0RL, England
Penguin Group Ireland, 25 St. Stephen's Green, Dublin 2, Ireland
(a division of Penguin Books Ltd.)
Penguin Group (Australia), 250 Camberwell Road, Camberwell,
Victoria 3124, Australia
(a division of Pearson Australia Group Pty. Ltd.)
Penguin Books India Pvt. Ltd., 11 Community Centre, Panchsheel Park,
New Delhi—110 017, India
Penguin Group (NZ), 67 Apollo Drive, Rosedale, North Shore 0632,
New Zealand (a division of Pearson New Zealand Ltd.)
Penguin Books (South Africa) (Pty.) Ltd., 24 Sturdee Avenue,
Rosebank, Johannesburg 2196, South Africa

Penguin Books Ltd., Registered Offices: 80 Strand, London WC2R 0RL, England

© 2009 by SD Entertainment, Inc. Based on video games published by Humongous,
Inc. Licensed by Humongous, Inc. Used under license by
Penguin Young Readers Group. All rights reserved. Published by
Grosset & Dunlap, a division of Penguin Young Readers Group, 345 Hudson Street,
New York, New York 10014. GROSSET & DUNLAP is a trademark of
Penguin Group (USA) Inc. Printed in the U.S.A.

Library of Congress Control Number: 2008022320

ISBN 978-0-448-45071-1   10 9 8 7 6 5 4 3 2 1

Chapter One

Tony Delvecchio, the center for the Penguins, sped down the ice and skated across his own blue line with the puck. As he entered the neutral zone he cut sharply to his left, controlling the puck with his stick and picking up speed.

Tony spotted his left wing, Vicki Kawaguchi, and fired a blazing pass toward her. Vicki took control of the puck with her stick just before she crossed the red line at center ice into the zone of the Penguins' opponents, the Panthers.

Tony and Vicki, along with their Penguins teammates, Joey MacAdoo, Ernie

Steele, Pablo Sanchez, and Achmed Kahn, were playing hockey against a team of their friends—Ricky Johnson, Arthur "A.C." Chen, Dante Robinson, Samantha "Sam" Pearce, Pete Wheeler, and Marky Dubois—who called themselves the Panthers. So far, Tony had led the Penguins to a great season, but they were currently trailing the Panthers by a single goal.

Tony knew he needed to work quickly if the Penguins were going to pull out a win, so he followed Vicki across the Panthers' blue line. Ricky, the Panthers' right wing, skated up to Vicki and reached for the puck with his stick. At the same moment, Sam, the Panthers' right defenseman, joined Ricky to double-team Vicki.

"Vicki, behind you!" Tony shouted.

Before Ricky could complete his swipe of the puck, Vicki flicked a short pass back to Tony in the faceoff circle to the left of the

Panthers' goal.

Guiding the puck
with a light touch
of his stick, Tony
skated around
Ricky, then
past Sam.
Marky, the
Panthers' left
defenseman, crossed the ice and
caught up with Tony as he approached the
Panthers' goal.

Skidding to a stop and sending up a
spray of ice with his skates, Tony fired a
cross-ice pass to his teammate Joey. Joey
then sped toward the Panthers' goal.

Pete, the Panthers' goaltender, skated
forward, setting himself up to block the shot
he was certain would be coming from Joey.
But at the last second Joey sent a return
pass speeding back to Tony, who had come

streaking across the front of the goal.

With a lightning-quick shot, Tony slapped the puck to the left of Pete and into the Panthers' goal. The red light behind the goal flashed and the goal buzzer blared loudly.

"Goal, Penguins!" the referee, Vinny Delvecchio, shouted, skating over and retrieving the puck. "Penguins 4, Panthers 4."

As Vinny skated out to center ice, Tony slid up next to him, matching his pace stride for stride.

"Nice shot, little bro," Vinny said without actually turning to look at Tony.

"Thanks, Vinny," Tony replied, thrilled by his brother's praise. "That's my third goal today."

"I can count, you know," Vinny said. "And don't get arrogant."

"I'm just telling it like it is, Vinny," Tony

replied. "Great is great."

Vinny shook his head and stopped at center ice. Four years older than Tony, Vinny played on his own hockey team, but he also enjoyed refereeing games for his younger brothers and sisters.

"Good stuff! Way to tie it up, Tony!" said Ernie, the Penguins' left defenseman, as he headed over to his position in the Penguins' defending zone. "Or should I call you 'the Scoring Machine'!"

Tony laughed. He knew he was good.

"Let's play!" Vinny shouted, skating into the faceoff circle at center ice.

Only minutes remained in the tie game.

Tony lined up in the circle opposite Dante, the Panthers' center, ready for the faceoff. Vinny stood between the two players, holding the puck at shoulder height.

Vinny dropped the puck into the center

of the circle, and Tony and Dante battled
for control. Their sticks slapped the ice,
clacking against each other until Tony
finally got the puck and skated it into the
Panthers' zone.

Shifting his stick to the front of the puck,
Tony flicked a pass back toward Pablo, the
Penguins' right defenseman. But A.C., the
Panthers' left wing, intercepted the pass
and streaked toward the Penguins' goal.

Joey picked up A.C. as he crossed into
the Penguins' zone, and Pablo also hustled

back to help out. A.C. fired a pass across the ice to Dante, who gathered in the puck. Then Dante drew back his stick and fired a slap shot at the Penguins' goal.

Achmed, the Penguins' goaltender, reached across the mouth of the goal and smacked the puck away with his stick.

"Nice save, Achmed!" shouted Ernie as he took the rebound and skated back up the ice.

Crossing the red line, Ernie spotted Vicki open on his right. He flipped a pass to her, but before she could gain control, Ricky had his stick next to hers, battling Vicki for the puck.

The puck was knocked free and slid toward the Panthers' blue line. Both Panthers' defensemen, Sam and Marky, raced toward it. But Tony streaked in from out of nowhere, skating between the two defensemen. He snatched the puck with his stick and barreled toward the Panthers' goal.

Drawing back his stick he fired the puck right at the goal. It whizzed past Pete, who flopped to the ice trying to make a stick save. The puck slammed into the net at the back of the goal just as time ran out.

Vinny blew his whistle. "Final score: Penguins 5, Panthers 4," he shouted. The Penguins had now won their first three games of the new hockey season. Everyone on the team cheered. It had been an exciting game.

"Good game, Tony," Sam said, offering a fist bump. "I don't know if we'll ever beat you guys as long as you're on the team."

"Four goals in one game, including the game winner," Marky added. "You really are something, Tony."

"Yeah, I guess I am, aren't I?" Tony replied, smiling and accepting high fives from his teammates.

"Hey, hot shot, I have to go," Vinny said,

skating toward the side of the rink. "I have my own game, and it starts in half an hour. I'll see you at home. Nice game, little bro!"

"Thanks, Vinny," Tony said, beaming.

"Yeah, thanks, Vinny," Ernie repeated. "You know, if you need one of us to ref your game with the older kids, I got a striped shirt for my birthday. It looks good, too!"

"We got it covered, kid," Vinny replied, laughing. Then he skated off the ice.

"Man, you made me look like I was a piece of Swiss cheese out there, Tony," Pete said as he peeled off his goalie's mask and pads.

"Don't worry about it, dude," Achmed said, patting Pete on the back. "Tony has a killer slap shot. He does the same thing to me at practice. I feel like I'm always checking my stick for holes after I go up against him."

"Hey, I'll see you guys at practice

tomorrow," Tony said, skating toward the side of the rink.

"Do you think you want to be seen practicing with us mere mortals?" Vicki asked jokingly.

Tony spun around, skating backward. "I won't tell anyone if you don't," he said, winking. Then he headed off the ice.

Chapter Two

"Okay, Vicki, Pablo, let's try that fast-break passing play again," Tony said to his teammates the next day at the Penguins' practice. "Remember not to cross the blue line into the attacking zone before the person with the puck, which will be me. Achmed, you're in the goal."

Achmed slipped on his mask and skated to his position in front of the goal.

"Take it easy on Achmed," Ernie shouted as he practiced skating and controlling the puck with this stick. "We need him in one piece for our next game."

"I think he'll survive," Tony replied,

lining up the puck at center ice. He turned to Vicki on his left, then Pablo on his right. "Ready?" Both players nodded.

The three Penguin players began skating toward the blue line. Both Vicki and Pablo were careful not to get ahead of Tony who controlled the puck. They knew that during a game, if they entered the opposing team's zone before their teammate brought the puck in they'd be called for an offside penalty.

Tony crossed the blue line first, with Vicki and Pablo trailing close behind. "Go!" Tony shouted.

Pablo sped up, pounding the ice with his skates, streaking ahead of Tony. Tony fired a pass toward Pablo who caught up to the puck and trapped it with his stick. Moving his stick from one side of the puck to the other to maintain control, Pablo closed in on Achmed who crouched in the goal.

At the same time, Vicki crossed to a spot just in front of the goal. Pablo whipped a pass right to her stick. She stopped the puck, drew back her stick, and fired a shot at the goal.

Achmed dropped down to the ice and whacked the puck away with his stick.

"Nice save, Achmed," Tony said. "Vicki. Instead of stopping the puck, then taking your shot, try to just redirect the puck right into the goal all in one motion. That makes it tougher for the goalie to pick up the angle of the shot."

"Gotcha," Vicki replied.

"Let's try it again," Tony said as the three friends skated back to center ice.

After working on the fast break a few more times, Tony skated over to Joey and Ernie. They were doing passing drills together.

"Let's work on some defense," Tony suggested.

"Okay," Ernie said, leaning forward with a serious look on his face. He placed his stick next to the puck, ready for action.

"Uh, Ernie, I meant *you* work on defense and I'll handle the puck," Tony explained.

"Oh. I knew that!" Ernie said, passing the puck to Tony.

"Okay, stop me from getting past you," Tony told Ernie.

"I could tackle you," Ernie pointed out.

"That would stop you."

"Right, and it would also give you a close-up look at the penalty box," Tony said, smiling. "Save the tackling for football. Just block my path and go after the puck with your stick."

Tony skated toward Ernie, who skated backward, keeping his eyes on every move Tony made. Tony moved his stick and the puck quickly to his left. Ernie skated in that direction to follow.

But Tony cut back swiftly to his right, catching Ernie moving the wrong way. He skated around Ernie before Ernie could recover.

"You need to focus

on my lower body and my skates," Tony explained. "I can fake you out with my stick, but I can't go anywhere my skates don't go. That's the key to blocking my path."

"How would your skates like to come with me?" asked a voice from across the rink.

"Vinny!" Tony exclaimed, skating over to his brother. "What are you doing here?"

"Can't a guy come to watch his little bro practice?" Vinny replied, leaning over the railing.

"You never came to watch my practice before," Tony said, curious about what his brother might be up to.

"That's because I haven't seen you play in a long time," Vinny replied. "When I reffed that game I got to see how good you've become. And you really are good."

"Thanks, Vinny," Tony said. "But I know you. You didn't come all this way just to tell me I was good, even though it's the truth."

"You're humble, too, I see," Vinny joked.

"Vin-ee!" Tony whined, realizing that he sounded like a little kid. "Will you tell me what's up?"

"Seriously! The suspense is killing *me!*" Ernie chimed in.

"How'd you like to try playing with my team?" Vinny finally asked.

Tony felt as if he were suddenly floating above the ice. "You're kidding, right?" he said. "You're just goofing on me, aren't you? Just busting my chops."

"I don't kid around when it comes to my hockey team, little bro. We're always looking for good players, and I liked what I saw the other day. But, if you're not interested . . ." Vinny turned and started to walk away.

"Whoa! Whoa!" Tony shouted. "Who said I'm not interested?"

Vinny turned back around and extended his hand. "So does that mean you're in?"

Tony grabbed his brother's hand and shook it briskly. "I'm in, big bro. I am *so* in!"

"You know you're not going be the best player out there anymore, hot shot," Vinny explained. "But playing with better players will help you bring your game up to the next level."

"Oh, I get it," Tony replied quickly, not wanting to give Vinny any excuse to take back his offer. "I'm good with not being the best. I'm going to learn so much from the older guys. It'll be awesome, Vinny. I am so psyched!"

"Sweet," Vinny said. "I'll see you at practice tomorrow. Don't be late."

"Whoo-hoo!" Tony yelled when Vinny had left. He sped down the ice, feeling like he was flying. He unleashed a monster slap shot that traveled the length of the rink, slammed into the board on the far end, and slid halfway back.

"Did you hear that, guys?" Tony said when he had skated back to his teammates.

"Hear what?" Ernie replied, unable to resist giving Tony a hard time. "Did somebody say something?"

"I can't believe I'm getting to play with Vinny's team," Tony said, skating back and forth across the ice, bursting with excitement. He came to a sudden stop in front of his friends when he noticed their disappointed faces.

"Well, I hope you remember us little people when you go off to the big time, 'hot shot.'" Vicki said.

"Vicki has a point," Joey added. "Does this mean you're dumping us? Are the Penguins going to have to play without their superstar?"

"Hey, guys, no worries!" Tony said. "I can handle being on both teams. It gives me twice as much time on the ice, and it's only going to make me a better player, so the Penguins will rock even more than we do now!"

"Killer, dude," Achmed said, giving Tony a high five. The rest of the Penguins looked just as relieved.

"I'm going to play with Vinny's team," Tony said quietly to himself, taking off and skating around the edge of the rink, unable to stand still any longer. "Wow!"

Chapter Three

Tony was excited and nervous as he skated onto the rink where his brother's team, the Seals, were getting ready to start their practice. He had barely slept the night before, going over plays and shots in his head in preparation for this practice. He could still hardly believe that he was on the same ice as Vinny, about to play for his big brother's team.

"*There* he is!" Vinny shouted, catching sight of Tony. "Come over here and meet the guys."

"Everybody, this is Tony, my little bro," Vinny announced, putting his arm around

Tony's shoulder. "But you can call him 'hot shot'!"

"Um, you can just call me Tony, actually," Tony said, a little embarrassed.

"This is Steven, our center," Vinny continued.

"How ya doing, Tony?" Steven asked.

"And this is Freddie, our left wing."

"What's up?"

"And Mack, our left defenseman."

"Dude."

"And this is Paul, our goalie."

"Vinny says you're good," Paul said. "I'm looking forward to seeing it."

"I play right wing, Tony," Vinny explained. "And you'll be our right defenseman."

"Uh, I usually play center," Tony said sheepishly.

"Hey, you're in the big leagues now, little bro," Vinny said. "You leave the scoring to me and Steven and Freddie. You just worry about defense for now. All right, enough talk. Let's play some hockey!"

Tony was relieved to finally get to work, although he was anxious about playing an unfamiliar position. *Defenseman? Why did Vinny pick me to play defense for his team, when he knows that scoring is my game?* Tony worried to himself.

The team lined up to run some drills.

Paul took his place in the goal, Tony and Mack took their positions just across their own blue line, and Vinny, Steven, and Freddie lined up at the red line facing them.

Steven skated forward with the puck and then fired a crisp pass to Vinny. Vinny crossed the blue line into the attacking zone and Tony immediately came out to meet him.

Tony skated right up to Vinny who cut to his right, then accelerated and blew right past Tony. Vinny reared back and launched a high slap shot. Paul reached out and caught the streaking puck in his goalie's glove.

"Nice glove save, dude!" Mack cried.

"So, Tony," Vinny began. "I know you're new at defenseman so let me help you out. If you get too close to the guy with the puck, like you did to me, it's easy for him to skate around you. Then you leave your goalie wide open and all alone. If you stay back a bit, you can cut off all his angles to the goal. Got it?"

"Got it," Tony replied, though he wasn't completely sure he had gotten it. As the Penguins' center and top player he was used to always being aggressive, always skating hard and pushing forward. He'd have to get used to playing back and waiting for the action to come to him.

"Okay, let's try it again," Vinny said.

The Seals lined up to repeat the drill. This time it was Steven who took the puck and tried to skate past Tony. Trying to follow his brother's advice, Tony backed up, staying with Steven.

Steven cut sharply to his left. Tony stayed right with him. But when Steven cut back to his right, he simply outskated Tony, got past him, and fired a shot, which got past Paul and flew into the goal.

"Better, little bro," Vinny said.

"Yeah, but he still got past me," Tony pointed out.

"That's just a matter of speed," Vinny explained. "You didn't do anything wrong."

This isn't going to be as easy as I imagined, Tony thought. *I'm used to being the fastest guy on the ice. But all of these guys are way faster than me. What did I get myself into?*

The practice continued. Tony worked hard to get more comfortable, though at times he felt as if he were moving in slow motion. He began to wonder if playing with Vinny's team was such a good idea.

"Let's try some shooting practice," Vinny said.

The Seals all lined up to practice their slap shots while Paul defended the goal. As Tony skated to the back of the shooting line he overheard Mack whisper to Vinny. "I

thought you said the little squirt was really good."

"Give him some time," Vinny replied. "He's got a lot of talent."

Tony was relieved to hear his brother standing up for him, but he knew he'd have to earn the respect of the rest of the team if he wanted to keep playing with them.

Vinny shot first. He fired a blazing slap shot that Paul deflected with his skate.

Mack shot next, skating toward the goal, then flipping the puck into the air, trying to sneak it over Paul's shoulder. Paul made a great glove save.

Both Steven and Mack fired hard slap shots, but Paul deflected each one with his stick.

Then it was Tony's turn. He took a deep breath and focused. *Shooting is what you do*, he said to himself. *Just do it!*

He drew his stick back then whipped it forward, slamming a powerful slap shot toward the goal. Paul reached down, but the puck sailed over Paul's shoulder and into

the net. Tony was the only one on the team to score against Paul during that drill.

"Not bad, squirt," Mack said.

Tony breathed a sigh of relief. He glanced over at Vinny who simply winked at him.

Maybe this is going to be okay after all, Tony thought.

"Okay, let's work on some stick handling," Vinny said.

The players all skated to one end of the rink. Then two by two they skated the length of the ice. One player in each pair controlled the puck. The other followed him the way an opponent would, trying to steal the puck.

When Tony's turn to control the puck came, he was paired with Mack. Tony skated up the ice quickly, shifting the puck from one side of his body to the other. Mack matched his skating, stride for stride, poking at the puck with his stick. But Tony maintained possession, keeping the puck away from Mack, skillfully handling his stick. He reached the far end of the ice with the puck still firmly in his control.

"That's some nice stick handling, squirt," Mack said. "Maybe Vinny's right about you after all."

The two players then switched roles for the return trip back down the ice. Mack handled the puck, with Tony playing the part of his opponent.

Mack took off quickly and Tony tried his best to keep up. He wasn't used to skating backward for such a long period of time, but he maintained his distance and tried to poke the puck away from Mack. Tony felt like he was doing all right until, about halfway down the ice, Mack seemed to kick himself into overdrive and skated right past Tony.

Tony slammed his stick to the ice in frustration.

"Hey, take it easy," Vinny said, skating over to Tony. "You're not going to get it all in the first practice. Relax. It'll come. Let's wrap it up for today guys. Three laps. Let's go!"

The Seals all took off. Tony lagged behind as they skated around the outside of the rink.

"Not bad, little bro, for a first practice," Vinny said, dropping back beside Tony. "But tomorrow at practice—no more taking it easy on the new kid." Then Vinny skated ahead to join his friends.

They were taking it easy on me? Tony thought. *Oh, great! What will tomorrow be like?*

Completing his third lap, Tony stepped from the ice, quickly changed into his sneakers, and grabbed his gear bag.

"See you guys tomorrow!" he shouted as he headed for the exit. "And thanks!"

"Don't be late!" Vinny called back.

"No way!" Tony cried as he slipped out the door, on his way to practice with the Penguins.

Once outside, Tony glanced at his watch and realized that he had five minutes to make the ten-minute walk to the rink where the Penguins held their practice. He broke into a run. *Speaking of being late!* he thought to himself. *I don't want to be late to the Penguins' practice. Although a nice two-hour nap would feel great right about now. I'm wiped.*

Running hard all the way, Tony arrived at the rink only a few minutes late. Bursting through the doors, he saw Joey lacing up his skates and joining his teammates on the ice.

"You made it," Joey said as Tony dropped his gear bag, yanked off his sneakers, and quickly pulled on his skates. "But just barely. I thought we'd have to start the practice without you."

"Hey, you guys know I'd never let you down," Tony replied, grabbing his stick and heading onto the ice.

"Too bad," Ernie said. "I was looking forward to being the hot shot. I figured it was my turn."

"No," Tony laughed. "It's still your turn to be the lukewarm shot. How's that?"

"Hey, you may be funnier than Vinny and his friends, but I'm the funny one around here," Ernie jokingly complained. He fired a pass to Tony.

"Trust me, dude," Tony replied, redirecting the puck toward Vicki. "There is nothing funny about Vinny or his friends. Those guys are incredible!"

"What happened to you being the hot shot?" Vicki asked, catching the puck and firing a shot at Achmed in the goal. He slapped the shot aside with a stick save.

"Oh, man, playing with those guys is

like the first day of school for me," Tony explained. "I've got so much to learn. But they've got practice again tomorrow, so I have a chance to work on my skills before our first game."

"Don't worry, Tony," Pablo said, recovering the puck and firing back to Tony. "You'll help them. I'm sure of it."

"Yeah, well, don't forget, we've got practice tomorrow, too," Joey reminded Tony.

"I know, Joey," Tony replied. "Like I said, I'd never let you guys down. Now enough talk. Let's play some hockey!"

The Penguins practiced hard for another hour. That evening when Tony got home, he was more exhausted than he had ever been before in his life. He ate his dinner, went to his room, and immediately fell into a deep sleep.

Chapter Four

Tony woke up the following morning and thought, *Gotta be at Seals' practice at 10.* He glanced at the clock. It read 9:45. It took a moment for this fact to register in his still sleepy mind, but when it did, he bolted from bed and dashed to his closet. Throwing on his clothes and grabbing his hockey gear, Tony ran from the house.

As team captain, Vinny always got to the rink before everyone else, so he had left the house long before Tony woke up.

I can't be late, Tony thought. *I'd never hear the end of it from Vinny.*

Already sweating when he hurried inside,

Tony saw Vinny and the others starting their warm-up skate.

"What happened to 'No way I'll be late,' Sleeping Beauty?" Vinny shouted as Tony scrambled into his skates, gloves, and helmet.

"Sorry, Vinny," Tony said, hurrying onto the ice. "I'm ready."

"Good," Mack said. "Because we're going to practice the three-on-two fast break again. And you and me are the two."

Tony and Mack took up their positions in front of Paul, who set himself in the goal. Vinny, Steven, and Freddie set up at the red line and began skating forward.

Stay back on the skater with the puck, Tony reminded himself. *Don't get fooled like yesterday.*

Steven started with the puck. He fired a pass to Vinny who picked up speed and skated right at Tony. Across the ice, Freddie streaked toward the goal, but he was met by Mack.

Tony followed Vinny's skates with his eyes, just as he had told Ernie to do during the Penguins' practice. Then he caught sight of Steven out of the corner of his eye. Steven skated right for the middle of the ice and Tony could see the play taking shape in his mind before it happened.

Tony backed away from Vinny just as Vinny drew back his stick and rocketed a pass toward Steven. But Tony had anticipated this move and slid his stick between them, stopping the puck. He then fired it back in the other direction, away from the goal.

"Now you're starting to think like a defensemen!" Vinny said. "Nice play."

"You know, Vinny," added Mack. "The little squirt might work out after all."

Tony felt his confidence growing. On the

next play, he was skating up the ice with
the puck, looking for an open teammate.
He spotted Steven up ahead. But he was so
focused on making a good pass, he didn't
notice Freddie sneaking up beside him.
Freddie hit Tony hard with a body check,
separated him from the puck, grabbed
the puck, and headed back in the other
direction.

"Hey!" Tony shouted, turning and skating
hard to catch up with the play. "That was a
hard hit!"

"But a clean one, kid!" said Freddie as he fired a shot past Paul. "What's the matter, don't they check hard in the kiddie league?"

"Leave him alone, Freddie," Vinny said. Then he turned to Tony.

"Freddie's right, little bro," Vinny added. "It was a clean check. You're gonna have to get used to that."

Tony knew that Vinny was right. He also now knew that he was going to have to get used to not just a faster game, but a more physical one, too, if he was going to help this team.

The longer the practice went on, the better Tony played. With the Seals' next game just days away, he was hoping he'd feel ready when the whistle blew and the action was for real.

"All right, let's run one more drill," Vinny announced. "It's almost one o'clock, so we should wrap it up soon."

"One!" Tony shouted. "Is it really that late?" He had been so focused on keeping up with his Seals teammates that he completely lost track of time.

"Yeah, so what's the problem, Tony?" Vinny asked.

"I gotta go," Tony replied, heading off the ice. "I was supposed to be at the Penguins' practice an hour ago. The guys are expecting me!"

"Hey, what about us, squirt?" Mack said, clearly annoyed. "I thought you wanted to play with us."

"I do," Tony said, then he turned to his brother. "Vinny, I really do. It's just, you know, they're my friends. I-I, I really gotta go!"

"I went out on a limb for you, Tony, with these guys," Vinny shouted, pointing at his teammates. "And now you're cutting out of practice early. I mean, do you want to play with us or not?"

"I'm sorry, Vinny," Tony said, pulling off his skates and slipping on his sneakers. "I do want to play with you. I really do. This'll never happen again. I promise."

Then Tony dashed from the rink.

Tony ran the whole way from the Seals' rink to the Penguins' rink. *Great, now Vinny's mad at me. Nice work, Tony. You managed to tick him off after he stood up for you to his teammates. How am I ever going to make this two-team thing work out?*

Bursting through the doors, he saw his teammates were wrapping up their practice.

"Hey, nice of you to show up, hot shot!" Joey shouted. He was practicing skating from one end of the ice to the other with the puck. "We're into our final drill here. What gives?"

"I'm so sorry, guys," Tony said, yanking off his sneakers and lacing up his skates.

"Practice with Vinny's team was so intense that I just lost track of time!"

"Oh, we understand, don't we, guys?" Vicki said as she took a pass from Ernie and fired a shot toward Achmed in the goal. "He was busy with his *new* team."

"Come on, guys," Tony pleaded. "I'm here now. Let's get to work."

"You got anything left for us, Tony?" Ernie asked, firing a pass to Tony.

"Plenty!" Tony replied, taking the puck and skating toward the goal.

Pablo picked him up on defense. "So how was practice today with the older kids, Tony?" he asked.

"Tough, Pabs," Tony replied, changing direction and skating past Pablo. He fired a shot at the goal, which Achmed deflected with his stick. "Those guys are so fast. Really fast. You guys think I'm fast, but . . ."

"And humble," Ernie added.

"Oh, I felt plenty humble out there, Ernie. For real. When they hit you with a check it feels like you just got run over by a truck."

"I have to go, guys," Joey announced after a few more minutes of practice.

"Me too," said Achmed. Then the rest of the Penguins skated off the ice and began to unlace their skates.

"I'm sorry, guys," Tony said. He'd only been there for a few minutes and the practice was already over. "It won't happen again. I promise. I won't be late again. So are you still coming to watch me play in my

first game with the Seals?" He flashed his biggest smile.

"I don't know," Vicki said. "I may have to water my plants."

"Yeah, I may have to get a haircut," Ernie added.

"I may have to feed my goldfish," Achmed said.

"Come on, guys!" Tony pleaded.

"Yeah, we'll be there, hot shot," Joey said. "But we may be a little late."

"Funny, Joey," Tony said as he left the ice. "Real funny."

On his way home, Tony tried to figure out how he was going to juggle being on two teams at once. *I hate to let my friends down. I've been playing with them for years. But I really hate to let Vinny down, too. Oh, no, Vinny. I almost forgot. What am I going to say to Vinny when I get home?*

Tony slipped into his house and hurried

upstairs as quietly as he could, hoping to avoid Vinny.

No such luck. Vinny popped out from his room as Tony reached the top step.

"What's going on with you, Tony?" Vinny asked as his younger brother dropped his gear on the floor and slumped down on the top step.

"I didn't realize your practice would run so long," Tony said, though it sounded lame even to him. "And I didn't want to let my buddies down."

"What about letting me down?" Vinny asked. "I stood up for you with the guys. Most of them didn't even want you to try playing with us. But I told them to give you a chance. And now *you* look bad and *I* look bad. So, let me ask you again—do you want to play on my team or not? Don't do me any favors. If you want out, just say so. If you can't handle being on both teams—"

"I can do it!" Tony shouted. "I can handle being on both teams, Vinny. Just give me another chance."

"You got it, little bro," Vinny said, turning toward his room. "Just don't make me look bad again."

"I won't, Vinny," Tony said.

"And get some rest," Vinny added. "You look like you just got run over by a bulldozer. We need you to be sharp for the game."

Tony nodded and headed into his room. *Things were a lot easier when all I had to do was win games for the Penguins. Still, I'm going to make this work. I have to. First, though, I need about two weeks of sleep!*

Chapter Five

Tony arrived at the rink an hour early
for his first game with the Seals. He was the
first one in the arena. He suited up, grabbed
his stick, and began skating from one end of
the ice to the other, controlling the puck.

I can't be in two places at once, he
thought as he practiced his stick handling.
*I'm just going to focus on this game now.
That's it. I'll think about the Penguins' game
later today when that comes around. That's
the only way this whole thing is going to
work out.*

One by one, the other players filed
into the arena. Tony spotted his Seals

teammates and the members of the Sharks, the team they were about to play, putting on their gear on the sidelines.

Those Sharks look even bigger than the guys on the Seals! he thought. Then he took a deep breath. *Just stay focused!* he reminded himself.

"Now that's better!" boomed Vinny as he skated out to warm up. "First man on the ice. I like it, little bro!"

Tony nodded and continued his own warm-up.

A few minutes later, as both teams got ready to play, Tony spotted his friends from the Penguins taking their seats in the stands. He skated over to the side of the rink.

"Hey, guys, you made it!" he shouted. "Cool!"

"I'm here to watch you teach the big boys a thing or two," Ernie said. "And I do mean 'big.' Look at those guys, will you? What do they feed them?"

Vicki elbowed Ernie in the shoulder. "Nice," she said. "Why don't you put a little more pressure on him. What Ernie means is, good luck today."

"Yeah, good luck, Tony!" Pablo called out.

"Rock their world, hot shot!" Achmed added.

"Just don't forget we've got a game later," Joey said seriously.

"I'll be there, Joey," Tony replied. Then he skated back to his Seals teammates.

Tony settled in his position, ready for the start of the game. The Sharks controlled the opening faceoff and brought the puck into the Seals' zone. The Sharks' left wing skated toward the goal. Tony slid to his left to cut off the angle to the goal.

The left wing whipped his stick to the right, hoping Tony would go for the fake and move in that direction. But Tony stayed focused on the left wing's skates, which kept moving in a straight line. As the wing brought his stick back, Tony poked the puck free. It skidded across the ice, where Mack gained control and sent it zooming back in the other direction.

"Good one!" Vinny shouted, gathering in the puck with his stick, then carrying it across the red line. Vinny spotted Steven and fired the puck to him. Steven took control and brought the puck across the Sharks' blue line.

Steven sent a cross-ice pass to Freddie who whipped the puck right back at Steven. With a powerful swing of his stick, Steven redirected the puck with a hard slap shot that flew past the goalie's shoulder and into the net for the first goal of the game.

Seals 1, Sharks 0.

The Seals mobbed Steven, pounding him

on the back. Tony was right in the middle of the pack. For the first time, he felt like a real part of the team.

The Sharks once again took control of the faceoff and the action moved quickly into the Seals' zone. This time Mack pried the puck free and fired a pass across to Tony.

Tony skated hard, close to the boards. As Tony crossed his own blue line, the Sharks' center slammed into him with a hard body check. He went crashing into the boards, losing control of the puck and falling to the ice.

The Sharks' center took the puck and made a break right for the goal as Tony scrambled back to his feet. The center skated around Mack. All that now stood between the Sharks and the game-tying goal was Paul, the Seals' goalie.

Tony picked up speed, desperately hoping to get back and protect Paul before the Sharks' center could get his shot off. He was too late. The center reared back and unleashed a blazing slap shot that zipped past Paul's outstretched glove and slammed into the net at the back of the goal.

Seals 1, Sharks 1.

I just wasn't fast enough, Tony thought as he watched the Sharks celebrate. Vinny skated up to Tony and put his arm around his shoulder.

"Forget about it, little bro," Vinny said. "Stay in the game. Stay focused." Then he skated over to his position.

Both teams played well and Tony felt more comfortable with each defensive play he made. Still, a part of him missed playing center, like he did for the Penguins. He really wanted to get his stick on the puck and take a shot at the Sharks' goal. Midway through the final period, with the score still tied 1–1, he got his chance.

As Vinny and the Sharks' center battled for control of the puck in the Seals' zone, the puck shot loose right in front of Tony. Accelerating, he captured the puck and crossed his own blue line. He saw a fast-break play developing and kicked his skating into high gear.

With Freddie on his left and Steven on his right, Tony brought the puck across the red line. He fired a pass to Freddie who carried the puck across the blue line into the Sharks' zone. Tony and Steven crossed into the zone behind Freddie.

Freddie sent a pass skimming across the ice to Steven. Two Sharks' defenders swarmed on the puck, but Steven managed to get off a pass—to Tony who was wide open in front of the goal.

Tony stopped the puck, then drew back his stick and launched a blistering slap shot that scooted under the goalie's stick.

Seals 2, Sharks 1.

The Seals mobbed Tony. As his Seals teammates pounded him on the back, Tony looked into the stands hoping to catch his friends' reactions. He expected to see them on their feet, cheering wildly for him. But when he glanced at their seats Tony saw that his Penguins teammates were all gone. They had already left.

Of course, he thought. *They had to leave to get to their own game on time. And I have to get to that game on time, too! But what can I do? We still have five minutes left to play here!*

Skating back to his own end of the ice, Tony focused on helping his team hold the lead he had just given them. As the clock ticked down, the play got more intense. A hard check sent Tony into the boards, only this time he bounced back and maintained control of the puck.

With under a minute left, the action moved into the Seals' zone. Paul deflected two hard Sharks' slap shots. Tony gathered in the rebound of the second shot, turned, and started skating up the ice. Spotting

Vinny near their own blue line, Tony fired a pass ahead. But the puck never reached his brother.

The Sharks' speedy center cut in between Tony and Vinny and stole the puck. He skated right past Tony and fired a shot at the goal. Paul dove for the puck, but it sailed just over his glove and into the goal.

Seals 2, Sharks 2.

The clock ran out. The game was about to go into overtime.

Overtime! This is the last thing I need, Tony thought. *Now I'm really going to be late for the Penguins' game.*

The play went back and forth in the overtime period. Tony played well. He deflected a pass, threw a hard body check of his own, and kept the Sharks away from his goal. Seven minutes into the overtime, Vinny, Steven, and Mack found themselves in the Sharks' zone on a fast break.

Mack fed Vinny the puck and Vinny sent a lead pass just ahead of Steven who gathered it in and fired a speeding slap shot at the Sharks' goal. The Sharks' goalie got a piece of his stick on the puck, but it bounced across the goal line for the winning goal.

The Seals formed a crowd with Steven in the middle. They all jumped up and down, waving their sticks wildly. Tony felt great that the Seals had won their first game with him on their team. He knew he had made some mistakes, but he also knew he had helped his team.

"Nice game, little bro," Vinny said, giving Tony a high five.

Tony beamed, caught up in the joy of victory and his brother's praise.

"Yeah, you're not so bad, squirt," Mack added, slapping Tony's back. "Too bad your friends didn't stick around to see you win."

"My friends!" Tony cried, suddenly

remembering where he was supposed to be. "I have another game. Vinny, I gotta—"

"Go!" Vinny shouted. "It's okay. You did great here!"

Tony skated off the ice, switched into his sneakers, and dashed from the rink.

By the time Tony arrived at the rink where the Penguins were playing, the game was already in the final period. And the Penguins were down 3–0.

As Tony laced up his skates he watched Joey skate down the ice with the puck. When Joey noticed that Tony had arrived he called for time and skated over to the side of the rink.

"You're kidding me, right, Tony?!" Joey shouted. "We're in the third period and now you show up! What happened to 'I'll be there'?! We all came out to support you, and it was great to see you play with Vinny's team, but what were you thinking, just

blowing us off like that!"

"Joey, I'm really sorry," Tony replied
grabbing his stick and stepping onto the ice.
"We went into overtime. What could I do?"

"You could decide which team you're
really on!" Joey yelled. "We've been playing
here with five players on a side. When you
didn't show up, the Panthers were nice
enough to agree to play with four skaters
and a goalie so the sides would be even and

we could have some kind of a game."

"Well, you're back at full strength now," Tony said, flashing a smile, hoping to lighten the mood.

"Yeah, great," Joey grumbled, skating away.

Now Joey's mad at me, Tony thought as he joined his Penguins teammates. *I didn't know it would be so hard to play for both teams. Am I ever gonna figure out how to make it happen? Not now. Gotta focus on this game now.*

The Panthers brought all six of their players out onto the ice.

"I'm real sorry I'm late, guys," Tony said to his teammates. "But there's still time to win this thing."

"Maybe we should all chip in and buy you a watch," Vicki grumbled.

"You can have my watch, Tony," Ernie joked. "Except the battery ran out a week ago, so it always says 3:15. At least it's right twice a day."

"I deserve all that, guys, I admit. I messed up," Tony said.

"Let's play!" Joey shouted. He clearly wasn't in the mood for Tony's apology.

Play resumed and Tony settled into his familiar position as the Penguins' center. But something didn't feel quite right.

He carried the puck across the red line and was met by Dante, the Panthers' center. Tony picked up speed, skating hard to get around Dante, but Dante stayed right with him. Usually, when Tony played with the Penguins, he was the fastest guy on the ice.

Dante matched him step for step, then reached in with his stick and slapped the puck loose. A.C. gained control of the puck for the Panthers, skated into the Penguins' zone, and fired a slap shot past Achmed to make the score 4–0, Panthers.

What's wrong with me? Tony wondered. *I can outskate and handle the puck better than Dante any day of the week.*

Tony lost the faceoff to Dante and the Panthers once again took control of the puck.

Dante passed to A.C. who skated into the Penguins' zone. A.C. saw Ricky skating toward the goal and sent a pass zooming toward him. But Joey swooped in and stole the puck.

Joey sent a pass ahead to Vicki who fired the puck to Tony. Tony crossed into Panthers' ice, where he was met on defense by Sam. Spotting Pablo on his right, Tony sent a pass toward him, but Marky deflected the puck to A.C. who moved back in the other direction.

Three passes later, Ricky fired a shot past Achmed for the Panthers' fifth goal of the game.

I didn't even see Marky, Tony thought.

Time ticked down and the final buzzer sounded, giving the Panthers a 5–0 shutout.

As the teams left the ice, Ernie turned to Vicki. "There's a guy on our team who looks just like Tony," Ernie quipped. "That is, until he steps onto the ice."

"Very funny, Ernie," Tony snapped, upset at himself for letting his friends down. "I don't know what's wrong with me. I feel like I'm moving at half speed in a fog out there."

"You're trying to be in two places at once, Tony," Joey said. "And so you're not really in either place."

"I thought you guys were happy for me when I got to play with Vinny," Tony said quietly. He felt horrible. It was his fault they had lost, but his friends weren't being very fair. He was working so hard, and they didn't even seem to notice.

"We were," Vicki replied. "Only now it

feels like we've lost a teammate."

"I'm still on this team," Tony said. "And I can make this work. I just have to try harder."

Then Tony grabbed his gear and stormed out of the rink.

Chapter Six

Tony didn't sleep much that night. He was torn. He tossed and turned in bed trying to figure out how he could make everyone happy and still have fun playing hockey. *I could quit Vinny's team and just play with my friends. That's always been fun and it's kind of cool being the best player out there. But I'm learning so much playing with Vinny even though I have to work really hard. And I can't quit the Penguins. They're my best friends. I have to keep trying to figure this out. Maybe it'll get easier as it goes along.*

The next day at the Seals' practice Tony

was exhausted. Not only hadn't he slept well, but all the double practices and back-to-back games were really taking their toll. As the other Seals wrapped up their practice session, Vinny pulled Tony aside.

"You need to stay and work on your checking, little bro," Vinny said. "Your speed and defense are getting better, and that's great. But the level of physical play on this team is way above what you're used to. It makes you an easy target when you have the puck. And you need to add some hard body checks to take your defensive game to the next level."

I know Vinny's right, Tony thought. *But how do I tell him I'm already late for Penguins' practice—again! I can't. He doesn't want to hear it. I have to stay.*

"Sure, Vinny," Tony said, sighing.

Tony took the puck. He practiced avoiding body checks, and also maintaining control of the puck when Vinny checked him into the boards. Then Vinny took the puck and Tony practiced delivering hard checks and prying the puck away from his brother.

At the end of the extra hour of practice, Tony was asleep on his feet, but he felt he had learned something.

"That was great, Vinny," he said. "I could feel myself gaining more confidence both in giving and taking those hits."

"It's a big part of the game as you get older and play against bigger players," Vinny explained. "Good practice today, little bro. Don't forget our next game this Sunday at one o'clock."

"Don't worry, Vinny," Tony said, heading out the door. "I'll be there."

Tony hurried to the rink where the Penguins held their practice. *If these guys are still talking to me I'll be shocked!* He pushed open the door to the rink, but when he got inside the place was empty.

"Oh, no!" he said aloud, dropping his gear and slumping into a seat. "I missed the whole practice. Maybe I can still catch them at the Leaning Tower!"

Every Friday after practice the Penguins went out for a snack together at their favorite pizza place, the Leaning Tower of Pizza. Tony rushed to the restaurant and spotted his friends seated around a long table.

"Well, look who's here," Vicki said. "It's that guy who used to play on our team."

Tony pulled up a chair and saw that the group had already polished off a couple of pies. He was even later than he had thought.

"We have some lovely cold pieces of crust left if you like," Ernie said, holding up a crust and dangling it in front of Tony's face.

Tony slumped back in his chair and stared at the ceiling. He didn't know what to say.

"What's up with you?" Joey asked, sounded concerned. "You look horrible. Are you okay?"

"Vinny just spent the last hour slamming me into the boards," Tony explained.

"Do we get to do that next?" Vicki asked sarcastically.

"Sure, take your best shot, Vicki," Tony said sighing. "It couldn't possibly make me feel any worse than I do now."

Tony looked up and realized his friends didn't seem so angry anymore. They looked concerned instead.

"Dude, you're wearing yourself out," Achmed said.

"Achmed's right, Tony," Ernie added. "Leading a double life might work for a superhero, but not for a hockey player."

"You're right, Ernie," Tony said. "I feel like I'm being pulled in opposite directions at the same time."

"Well, that's one way of getting taller," Ernie quipped.

"Seriously, Ernie, I feel like I'm being split in two," Tony complained.

"So what are you going to do, Tony?" Pablo asked.

"Right now I'm going to go home and sleep," Tony said.

"Good idea," Joey said. "We're going to

need you to be sharp for our rubber game against the Panthers. It's Sunday at one."

Tony bolted out of his chair. "Sunday at one?" he cried. "But the Seals have a game Sunday at one!"

Tony fell back into his seat wishing he really could split himself in two. He wondered how in the world he was going to pull off being in two places at the same time.

Chapter Seven

All day Saturday, as Tony did chores around the house and caught up on schoolwork, he struggled to find a solution to his problem. He went out of his way to avoid Vinny. He really hadn't made up his mind yet and he didn't want to talk about either playing for the Seals or missing their game until he figured out what to do.

When he woke up Sunday morning, Tony grabbed his hockey gear and headed to the rink where the Seals were going to play their game. He suited up, laced up his skates, and starting to warm up by skating back and forth from one end of the ice to the other.

He pictured himself playing for the Seals in the game that day. Then he immediately thought about his friends on the Penguins. He imagined them arriving at their rink and doing their warm-ups, getting ready for their game against the Panthers. Then he thought about them waiting for him and wondering if he was going to show up.

Vinny arrived before the rest of his Seals teammates. Spotting his brother, Tony skated to the edge of the ice and stepped off.

"Hey, little bro, you're here early," Vinny said, putting down his gear. "Ready to kick some butt out there today?"

"Well, Vinny, that's what I need to talk to you about," Tony replied. "You see, our game starts at one."

"Tell me something I don't know," Vinny shot back.

"Well, the Penguins also have a game today," Tony explained. "And it also starts at one."

"When did you find this out?" Vinny asked.

"Friday," Tony replied.

"Why didn't you say anything to me yesterday?" Vinny asked. "I noticed you were acting a little weird. I mean, weirder than usual."

"Because I hadn't made up my mind about what to do."

"So, Tony," Vinny said, looking his brother right in the eyes. "What *are* you going to do?"

Chapter Eight

The Penguins skated around the outside
of their rink, warming up for the game
against the Panthers. The game was
scheduled to start in just a few minutes.

"Still no sign of Tony, huh?" Vicki asked
as she slid smoothly across the ice, switching
from one foot to the other.

"The dude never did tell us what he was
going to do," Achmed pointed out.

"Maybe he figured out how to split himself
in half, after all," Ernie suggested. "You
know, without getting all gross and stuff."

"Tony will come through," Pablo said
softly. "He won't let us down."

Warm-ups ended and the Penguins gathered at their end of the ice. Dante skated over from the Panthers' side of the ice.

"So what's up with Tony?" he asked. "Is he showing up or do we have to play five-on-five again?"

Joey glanced up at the clock. It read 12:58.

"Well, I guess Tony made his decision," Joey said sadly, looking down and shaking his head.

"Yes, I did," said a voice from behind Joey.

"Tony!" Joey cried, smiling. "You made it!"

"You bet," Tony said, slipping on his skates. "I thought about you guys out here playing without me and I just knew that I couldn't let my friends down. I made a commitment to all of you long before Vinny asked me to play with him. And even though I learn a lot of stuff from Vinny, it's way more fun to play with you guys."

"Does Vinny know yet?" Vicki asked.

"That's why I'm late," Tony explained. "I had to tell him what I decided."

"And what did he say when you told him?" Vicki asked.

"He was pretty cool about it actually," Tony explained. "He was disappointed, especially since he said he could see how much better I was getting. But he did say he respected me for my loyalty to my friends."

"Aw, Tony, I think I'm gonna cry," Ernie said, pretending to dab tears away from his eyes.

"Yeah, well, don't," Tony said. "You'll get the ice all slippery. Anyway, Vinny got a buddy from school to take my place today. He also made me promise that I would still practice with the Seals now and then and play in some games with them when the Penguins didn't have a game at the same time."

"Welcome back, Tony," Pablo said, smiling.

"Thanks, Pabs," Tony said. "Now who's

ready to go out and beat these guys!"

All six Penguins skated to their positions, ready for the opening faceoff. None of them had any doubts that they would beat the Panthers and win the rubber game of the series. Tony took his place as center and smiled. It felt good to be back where he belonged: on the ice with his best friends.